T0221874

POEMHOOD
OUR BLACK REVIVAL

Poemhood

Our Black Revival

History, Folklore &
the Black Experience:
A Young Adult Poetry Anthology

Edited by

Amber McBride, Taylor Byas & Erica Martin

HARPER TEEN
An Imprint of HarperCollinsPublishers

HarperTeen is an imprint of HarperCollins Publishers.

Poemhood: Our Black Revival
Copyright © 2024 by Amber McBride, Taylor Shalon Byas,
and Halcyenda Erica Martin
All rights reserved. Printed in the United States of America.
No part of this book may be used or reproduced in any manner whatsoever without
written permission except in the case of brief quotations embodied in critical articles
and reviews. For information address HarperCollins Children's Books, a division of
HarperCollins Publishers, 195 Broadway, New York, NY 10007.
www.epicreads.com

Library of Congress Control Number: 2023937022
ISBN 978-0-06-322528-2

Typography by David Curtis
23 24 25 26 27 LBC 5 4 3 2 1
First Edition

For you, *reader*, may your life be a poem and remember . . .

Folklore is the boiled-down juice, or pot-likker, of human living.
—Zora Neale Hurston

Introduction

Poemhood: Our Black Revival is a celebration—a homage to the beauty and musicality of Black poetry, folklore, and history. We often hear stories about Zeus, Hades, Rapunzel, or Cinderella, and nothing about Anansi, Adze, or John Henry, the man who hammered through a mountain faster than a drill. This exclusivity of story is also found in the poetry that is taught; Robert Frost and Edgar Allan Poe are "serious" poets who must be included in all curricula. We see these discrepancies in how "valuable" certain genres of music are—Bob Dylan is a poet, and Tupac was just making a bunch of noise. Black art, Black music, and Black culture are not given their flowers, and *Poemhood: Our Black Revival* attempts to highlight the brilliance and diversity of the Black experience.

This collection also lights a candle to and for the brilliant Black poets who are now ancestors. By placing poems written sixty years ago beside poems written today, words are able to reach across time and converse on the page. *Poemhood: Our Black Revival* weaves together a patchwork quilt of poetry that highlights and celebrates the Black experience—old and new.

These poets and poems speak to the eclectic Black experience and emphasize how it is not a monolithic culture, as is often taught in schools. In fact, it is quite the opposite; Black culture is vast—it stretches longer than the Nile and is four times as deep. Black experiences and traditions are complex, varied, and striking. Black people carry more than just unimaginable pain—there is also joy, laughter, and swagger.

Zora Neale Hurston once said, "Folklore is the arts of the people before they find out that there is any such thing as art." Indeed, for Black people, the oral tradition has always been a treasured art. It is widely known that the oral tradition predates the written word by thousands of years. For centuries, songs, stories, chants, and folktales were the primary tools used to remember and record African history.

In the 1500s, many Africans were stolen from their homelands and transported to the Americas, where they were enslaved and stripped of their traditions. Many of these enslaved people were not permitted to learn to read or write. It is because of their stories that we know much of what they endured. Their firsthand accounts, folklore, fairy tales, and old wives' tales were preserved because the oral tradition traveled across the ocean and took root in the New World. Many truths about the horrors of chattel slavery in the United States would have been forgotten in the retelling of history if it were not for the stories African Americans passed down from generation to generation. African American folklore, fairy tales, and old wives' tales are an important piece of the puzzle when attempting to document African American history in the United States accurately.

African American folklore is unique because it is constantly balancing African traditions experienced within a Eurocentric environment—there is a duality to it that remembers and reinvents. Some traditions and thoughts stay firm, though—the importance of water, community, and animals as symbols is seen in both African and African American folklore. Conversely, only in African American folklore do we see the retelling of biblical tales and images of African Americans sprouting wings and flying across the Atlantic.

Our goal with this anthology is to show it all—the devil at the crossroads, Orishas, hoodoo, pain, joy, frustration, community, and, most of all, at the center of every folktale—a universal truth. Too often Black narratives are called *not literary* because the magical aspects in them do not *fit* the Eurocentric mold for what is *literary*. Writers like Toni Morrison, Maya Angelou, Zora Neale Hurston, Lucille Clifton, and many more refused to fit in the box made by western society. Instead, they sawed out of the box and went walking into open pastures of possibility—they would not be silenced, and magic made their words glitter on the page.

What does a mermaid look like? If we simply relied on Eurocentric folklore and myth, which we usually do, a mermaid must have long flowing hair, pale skin, and giant blue eyes. Princesses are always locked away and need saving or protecting. These narratives never include Black folklore or African stories that are older than time, but *Poemhood: Our Black Revival* invites young adults into this lush world of folklore and the Black experience.

In this anthology, poets spanning generations lovingly reflect, inspect, comment, and retell many Black folktales. The poems remember and talk with the poems of those who came before, while offering fresh perspectives on current events. *Poemhood: Our Black Revival* is a lush collection of stories and experiences, and, of course, there are a few ghosts haunting the pages because, in Black culture, ancestors are ever present—their strength and legacy guide us long after they are gone.

Each poem will be accompanied by an outro, which serves to provide additional information and context for the poem's historical positioning and/or its creation.

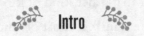

Young Afrikans

Gwendolyn Brooks

of the **furious**

Who take Today and jerk it out of joint
have made new underpinnings and a Head.

Blacktime is time for chimeful
poemhood
but they decree a
jagged chiming now.

If there are flowers flowers
must come out to the road. Rowdy!—
knowing where wheels and people are,
knowing where whips and screams are,
knowing where deaths are, where the kind kills are.

As for that other kind of kindness,
if there is milk it must be mindful.
The milkofhumankindness must be mindful
as wily wines.
Must be fine fury.
Must be mega, must be main.

Taking Today (to jerk it out of joint)
the hardheroic maim the
leechlike-as-usual who use,
adhere to, carp, and harm.

And they await,
across the Changes and the spiraling dead,
our Black revival, our Black vinegar,
our hands, and our hot blood.

Vol. 1: Livin'

We die. That may be the meaning of life. But we do language.
That may be the measure of our lives.
—Toni Morrison

Track 1: Power

Audre Lorde

The difference between poetry and rhetoric
is being ready to kill
yourself
instead of your children.

I am trapped on a desert of raw gunshot wounds
and a dead child dragging his shattered black
face off the edge of my sleep
blood from his punctured cheeks and shoulders
is the only liquid for miles
and my stomach
churns at the imagined taste while
my mouth splits into dry lips
without loyalty or reason
thirsting for the wetness of his blood
as it sinks into the whiteness
of the desert where I am lost
without imagery or magic
trying to make power out of hatred and destruction

trying to heal my dying son with kisses
only the sun will bleach his bones quicker.

A policeman who shot down a ten year old in Queens
stood over the boy with his cop shoes in childish blood
and a voice said "Die you little motherfucker" and
there are tapes to prove it. At his trial
this policeman said in his own defense
"I didn't notice the size nor nothing else
only the color". And
there are tapes to prove that, too.

Today that 37 year old white man
with 13 years of police forcing
was set free
by eleven white men who said they were satisfied
justice had been done
and one Black Woman who said
"They convinced me" meaning
they had dragged her 4'10" black Woman's frame
over the hot coals
of four centuries of white male approval
until she let go
the first real power she ever had
and lined her own womb with cement
to make a graveyard for our children.

I have not been able to touch the destruction
within me.
But unless I learn to use
the difference between poetry and rhetoric
my power too will run corrupt as poisonous mold
or lie limp and useless as an unconnected wire
and one day I will take my teenaged plug
and connect it to the nearest socket
raping an 85 year old white woman
who is somebody's mother
and as I beat her senseless and set a torch to her bed
a greek chorus will be singing in 3/4 time
"Poor thing. She never hurt a soul. What beasts they are."

⚹ ⚹ ⚹ ⚹

Outro: Clifford Glover was only ten years old when he was murdered by an undercover New York City police officer. The year was 1973, and the officer in question was later acquitted, which sparked riots in Queens, New York. This poem documents the rage, pain, and powerlessness the community felt after the acquittal of the officer. The vivid imagery throughout the poem forces the reader to experience the brutality Clifford was subjected to while also drawing attention to the lack of empathy, fairness, and justice offered to Black people in the United States.

Track 2: the South
Erica Martin

they'll hold the door for you
and direct you to your melanin-designated area
of society, with a firm nod
and a smile.

you'll thank them, as always, because
thank God for manners.

✳ ✳ ✳ ✳

Outro: In this poem about the Black experience of living in the
South, we see how restraint and injustice are and were a part of
everyday life. The irony here is that the South is known for its
manners, but racism is prevalent in the area. The two ideas don't
seem to mesh, and yet that is the reality. The speaker in this poem
is aware of this dichotomy—segregation and politeness holding
hands, the understanding being that Black people are not equal
and thus they should be happy with what they get, even if it is
separate and not equal.

Track 3: Colors

Fatima Stephens

Always told to pick a favorite,

Yet I never could.

Perhaps for the moment,

Or to match for the day,

But to pick one of such a wide array?

Each hue and shade a complement to each other.

A contrast or ballast.

Greens that defy yellow

Or sometimes blue

Shades of deep red

Singing violet I love yous.

Prisms radiating such brilliance

Our eyes can barely perceive.

Deceived to believe in eleven,

When in fact, there are eighteen decillion,

And of them,

Our eyes discern ten million.

White and light colliding,

To give the world pearlescent darlings.

Black taking ownership of all,

Devouring the light to feed them all their deserved shine.

How is it even possible to make a singular choice?

To choose only one

Is as abhorrent as choosing none.

⚜ ⚜ ⚜ ⚜

Outro: On the surface this poem appears to be about picking a favorite color. It should be a simple enough task—there are so many options. The poem reads like a list until there is a subtle shift in the final five lines, which imply that the color *Black* is powerful, but hardly ever given its due. Black is often seen as the absence of color or the shade that absorbs all other hues. Black deserves its time to shine with all the other colors of the rainbow.

Track 4: Textured
Kandace Fuller

A stroke of a hand
cast rivulets of shame and dissonance with each brush of a
   fingertip
the curled ringlets of my identity twist around every bent
   knuckle—
I was ashamed of this hair for far too long.

Taunting words of my childhood surround me like a pitfall
and drive me down an expanded road
of self-contempt.

nappy . . .
dirty . . .
unprofessional . . .

This slander and mockery ingrained in me a conditioned
   response.
A soldier bucking, weaving, and scrambling to avoid the
   discriminatory landmines scattered
through the battlefield.

Straighten it so you can fit in with the masses.

Don't color it or it won't seem real.

Have you ever seen anything more ghetto?

Twisted . . .

Braided . . .

Rows of healthy black corn . . .

Natural styles inherited from our ancestors were degraded
and demolished under the heavy weight of anger and jealousy.
A line forcibly forged the illusionary dichotomy between
    good and bad

The straighter, the better.

The curlier, the worse.

The kinkier, the most inferior you will ever be.

A stroke of a hand
cascades down with ignorant reverence, as if I were a prized
    breed in a cultural exhibition
a barrage of questions express unenlightened admiration and
    wonder as
unfamiliar fingers intimately caress every strand
of my pride.

You love this hair now that it is something we can no longer
   be shamed for.
Our familial styles, our cultural heritage, is fascinating enough
   to be embezzled,
plagiarized, and capitalized on, though it is still seen as

nappy . . .
dirty . . .
unprofessional . . .

Despite the negative looks,
despite the contradictory gazes,
despite the rejection of my kind of natural
I have never been prouder of my hair.

Don't touch it.

⚹ ⚹ ⚹ ⚹

Outro: Black natural hair is brilliant, but it has often been stigma-
tized as being "bad" or "unruly" by the mainstream media, where
Eurocentric features are the beauty standard. Many Black people
think they need to straighten, tug, and push their hair into styles
that tick the boxes for *good hair.* This poem is an ode to loving Black
hair! Black hair is versatile, it can be styled so many ways—braids,
straightened, twists, locs, and so much more.

Track 5: 10:32 p.m.

Courtne Comrie

I asked God three times to take this thorn away from me/but thorns keep the predators at bay/so instead/we preserve joy/ joy like Holy Ghost quick feet/like oxtail gravy/like laughing until your side splitting/like rent paid/like they graduated/ like the DJ said SHINE A LIGHT ON EM/like we cousins cause our Moms are friends/like a new birthday fit/like McDonald's after a doctor's visit/like *look who got a promotion/* like reunions/like clocking out before the sun sets/like 5 for 5 on anything/like baby shower food/like we all on the same Netflix account/like baby finally walking/like the bodega still open/like dental and vision included/like they home now/like they healed now/like we healed now/we healed now

✳ ✳ ✳ ✳

Outro: "10:32 p.m." is a prose poem about the collective joys found within the Black community in the midst of struggle. These small joys offer healing in their simplicity and uniqueness. These small joys speak to the importance of community, tradition, and love within the Black community. Even if the specific struggle itself hasn't disappeared or changed, small moments offer levity. The different "joys" listed are mundane and relatable to the reader, including "10:32 p.m."—a time we've all experienced.

Track 6: Views for Damani
Tony Keith Jr.

saw the blurry moon and Jupiter's blink
from my southeastern backyard after midnight
while looking through my telescope's lens -
best birthday gift thus far from my husband:
a man who prefers to keep his smooth and soft feet
inside of crispy clean sneakers that kiss concrete,
while I allow my toes to tingle between sweet sharp grass
that, during the day, be all slick and shiny from the sun,

which is up in the sky where Damani went
when the bullets that were shot into him
shattered hot metal into his blood full of iron,
making his spirit and his body heavy and tired,
causing him to fall asleep forever
on the cold concrete basement floor
inside of a house that he never lived in,
and that police say was a targeted break-in.

my ancestor is a nineteen-year-old Black boy
who wrote poems and read books and smiled at me

when saying his mother was beautiful,
as he explained the photographs of her
he taped to the wall of his barricaded room at juvie,
where I was teaching him to find freedom in poetry,
and reminding him how bright his light reflects
in every word he was writing inside that dark space
until he went home: free.

now, Damani's face is up there with the rest of them:
the eyes of people I love and will never see as flesh again;
the ones I never met, nor knew existed;
the ones that mixed the African brown
into the color, not race, of my Black American skin,
and their bright eyes, piercing through clouds,
casting shadows in circles around shades on the ground
where my Husband and I be standing,
staring at airplanes, pigeons, doves, cuckoos, rain,
fireworks, gnats, houseflies, carpenter bees, and balloons.

I bet they're all eager for us to look up sometimes,
just so we all see where we are as our earth rotates,
and yellow sunrays become golden sparkling stars
that we be down here wondering why they twinkle,
and what, not who, the names of some of them are.

what if they just want us to know:

there's more beneath the ground, than what's above it,

there's more behind the sky, than what's beyond it,

there's some infinite wisdom that's older than

human imagination, and Holy books, and dinosaurs;

there's some accessible source of divine knowledge

that's abundant, and rich, and thick, and clear,

but too big, too wide, too tall, and too complicated

for anyone who ain't up there

to hold onto down here.

perhaps what living people think to be true about

our entrance, existence, and exiting the world

ain't as great as the actual thing that's watching it all: It.

perhaps there's more Its who all watch over each other.

perhaps there's a select group of Its

and perhaps those particular Its don't fight,

or perhaps sometimes those Its do,

and perhaps that's when the people start dying;

. . . perhaps they needed Damani's perspective.

※ ※ ※ ※

Outro: "Views for Damani" is an attempt at answering infinite old questions about death: Why do we die? Where do we go? Regarding this poem, the author also added, *My husband gifted me a telescope for my forty-first birthday because he knows I am fascinated* *by the amount of stars I can see from our backyard. One night, while trying to find Jupiter, I learned that a young man I taught poetry to in a juvenile detention center, Damani Saunders, was released, and then later shot to death in the basement of somebody's house. I thought about the idea of heaven being up in the sky, where the stars are, and suggest that perhaps, metaphorically, they are the eyes of ancestors watching what's going on down here.*

Track 7: Greasy Butt Kids
Dr. Joanne V. Gabbin

My mother Jessie was one of the Greasy Butt Kids.
Don't laugh. There's a story in that.
She was the fifth of eleven-head of children
Born to Thomas and Elizabeth Smallwood,
Who believed in two religions: work and family.
One religion depended on the other.

From an early age the Smallwood children
Worked the land in Windsor, North Carolina,
Picking cotton, handing tobacco, raising hogs,
And keeping chickens.
They tilled and tended their own land,
And sharecropped for others in Bertie County.

Before the sun flushed the eastern sky,
Tommy, Biggie, Peenane, Ugabee, Jay,
Rayfield, Bus, Georgie, Jessie, Nellie, and Mae
Were kneeling in the red clay, pine needled fields.
Nellie, next to the youngest girl,

Sometimes stayed back to cook
The afternoon ration of field peas and ham hocks.

Schooling was cut short when the crops
Demanded their hands.
The Smallwood harvest was
Two generations of owning their own labor.
That fact didn't go unnoticed.
Those whose privilege lay in their white skin
Paid little mind to anything else.

Thomas was a trustee at Mt. Olive Baptist Church.
His erect sisters went to Normal School
And taught children to strive for more than the farm.
Elizabeth, a praying woman, was a healer and a midwife.
Her keeping shelf was loaded with pouches
Of goldenseal and sassafras root.
Black folks and white called on her night and day
For a laying on of hands.

They went about their lives in this uneasy sanctuary
Until it wasn't easy anymore.
Deacons in the church told Thomas to watch himself.
Poor whites didn't like that his children
Ate better than theirs.

Black men in the county had been strung
Like ornaments on tulip poplars for less.

Thomas, his chiseled jaw set slate sharp,
Fixed up the old rusty jalopy
And hid it in the woods until the time was right.
He left his home, his wife, and children
With the promise that he would return.
He made his way to the east side of Baltimore
And found a place to hold a new purpose.

Elizabeth and her children had to carry on.
The older ones looked after the young,
But they could not protect their mama from those
Who came looking to take away what was theirs.
When two angry white men called out, "Lizzie,
Give us the key to the smokehouse,
Or we gonna knock it down,"
Elizabeth calmly went inside the shotgun house,
Loaded the rifle Thomas had left,
And went back to the porch.

She said, "I done delivered your babies
And cared for your womenfolk.
You will not take food out of my chillen's mouths."

The pointed rifle gave them pause.
They left—for the time being,
But Elizabeth knew that they would be back.

Next morning, she sent her two oldest boys to Weldon
To board the colored train car headed North.
Tommy and Biggie found their father in Baltimore
And told him what was happening at home.
Thomas bought a black Model-T Ford
Large enough to fit his family.

He came at night with only a crescent moon
To light the country blue black dark.
In hushed hurriedness he woke the children
Told them to dress and go outside.
Thomas cleared the smokehouse of the hams hanging from
    hooks,
And Elizabeth stacked them at the bottom of the rumble seat.
The children piled in on top of them.

Everything else was left.
The pine beds and tables that he had built,
The knickknacks and doilies that Elizabeth
Showed off to her slant-eyed sisters-in-law,
The hogs in the pen and some hands

Of tobacco in the barn, and the chickens.
No time to fry a few for the journey.

When they arrived on Eager Street
On a morning in the late fall of 1930,
The neighbors saw the sleepy children
Unfold their cramped bodies from the car.
Their children, already lean from Depression diets,
Laughed loudly at the country kids
Who had grease spots on their skirts and pants.

From that day on the Smallwood kids
Were called "Greasy Butts."
But I'm telling you, they had the last laugh.
While other children simply made do,
They were the ones who had meat with their bread.

꙳ ꙳ ꙳ ꙳

Outro: The narrative arc of this poem highlights a colorful and radiant world where family is everything. Black life in the South is painted clearly in this poem while explaining the origin of the phrase *greasy butt kids*. A mother is forced to protect her family from white people who try to take what they think is theirs. This story is one that has played out in the South repeatedly, and has ended with the Great Migration north.

Track 8: Laughers

Langston Hughes

Dream-singers,
Story-tellers,
Dancers,
Loud laughers in the hands of Fate—
　My people.
Dish-washers,
Elevator-boys,
Ladies' maids,
Crap-shooters,
Cooks,
Waiters,
Jazzers,
Nurses of babies,
Loaders of ships,
Rounders,
Number writers,
Comedians in vaudeville
And band-men in circuses—
Dream-singers all,—

My people.
Story-tellers all,—
My people.
Dancers—
God! What dancers!
Singers—
God! What singers!
Singers and dancers
Dancers and laughers.
Laughers?
Yes, laughers . . . laughers . . . laughers—
Loud-mouthed laughers in the hands
Of Fate.

⚬ ⚬ ⚬ ⚬

Outro: This list poem reads like an ode to the Harlem Renaissance! It laughs in the face of adversity and celebrates the talents of Black folks. The best singers, dancers, and laughers. The extensive list in this poem emphasizes that the Black community is not a monolith, but rather a people capable of many pursuits, dreams, and talents. The power of this poem is in its perceived simplicity that actually is expansive.

Track 9: Like a Wildfire
Ashley Woodfolk

1.
Papa went first, when I was nine.
My mother's father. My brother's hero.
Tall and handsome and gentle,
deep-voiced and always honest,
a friendly giant from a storybook.

When we watched nature documentaries
he asked me who I was rooting for:
the hunter or the hunted.
I could never decide.
He told me that when it came to nature
there were no good guys or bad guys.
There were only those who lived
and those who didn't.

But I wanted everything to survive.

Stroke in his recliner.
Kids (like me) rushed from the room.

Then cancer, slow and deliberate as his handwriting
pulling him apart, like a vulture.

How could I walk into his house without him there
big and burly in his recliner?
How could I sit at his table without his fingers scurrying like
    a spider across it to tease me,
scurrying away when I smashed his hand with mine,
like any part of him was something
I could kill?

At his funeral, I laughed with my cousin.
We were little and didn't know how to sit
with so much sadness.

His absence hovered.

Like a storm cloud.

2.
Grandma went next. My father's mother.
The sweetest, loudest mother-in-law
for my sweet, loud mother.
Pain switching sides of the family
like to take another from the same bloodline
too soon would be too much.

(It was always too much.)

Her hair was thin, and her smile was wide,
and she was always yelling about something
while trying to feed me.
I loved her wood-burning stove,
the crooked one-story house my grandpa built with his own
    hands,
the dusty photos all over her shelves.
The way she'd say my name in her southern lilt,
drawing out the *A* like it was the beginning of a song.

She'd pet me with her hard hands,
like everything about me was soft, precious.
And she was pocket-sized—so small that I wish I'd tucked
    her into the jacket I was wearing
when I saw her at the hospital without realizing it was the
    last time.

I was older then.
More understanding of the permanence.
Understanding that my grandmother's rough smoker's voice,
her rougher hugs
would never be heard or felt again.

At her funeral I cried, but only once.

Like a sun shower.

3.

Losing Granny hit different.
My mother's mother.
A mother to so many mothers.

Chocolate-skinned and white-haired,
like Storm from X-Men if she'd been an old lady.
And maybe Granny was a mutant, a superhero.
She was certainly superhuman.

She could change my mood the way Storm changed the weather
with a joke, with a story,
with her fingers as they worked to untangle my thick, woolen
     hair.
She'd make me dinner and make me dance
while she swung her hips, and pursed her lips
singing over the stove in her too-hot kitchen.

Dimples like coin slots in either cheek,
as if the universe knew, when it was stitching her together,
that her attention was a prize everyone would pay to win.

Alzheimer's stole her from us in pieces,

a puzzle that began
to look and feel and be less and less like itself
until she'd nearly (and then completely)
disappeared.

I cried for weeks.
I got a tattoo.
I wrote her into book after book. Poem after poem.
Even now if I see a brown-skinned woman with white hair
or bowed legs
or dimples
or if I hear something that reminds me of the high twist of
  her laugh
I'll be lost in it again, the losing her.
The weight of it threatening to pull me under.

Like a stone in water.

4.
And then there was Grandpa.
My kind father's kinder father.
Strong and silent. Unknowable and noble.
The one I knew least.
He gave us his name, but never let anyone see into his
  heart.

When he drank, he cracked jokes and shoved shoulders.
Seemed more settled and at peace in his own skin.
And loving that peace was what ultimately took him:
his body forgetting how to recognize itself without
the sweet and sour pickling of booze.

But even sober his attachment to us was bright and absolute.
Hot and hungry.
Wordless and windowless as he was,
his love left nothing,
not even doubt,
in its wake.

Like a wildfire.

5.
And now there is me.
My moods like storm clouds.
My tears like sun showers.
My grief heavy as a stone in water.
My life brilliant and always burning.

A phoenix rising from their ashes.

※ ※ ※ ※

Outro: Grief is heavy. Each encounter with it leaves us fundamentally changed. This poem traces the arc of grief, it tracks the change, the growth, the memory. It writes loved ones into story, which immortalizes them. The cost of love may be pain when the loved one departs, but it is always worth it. Our ancestors always rise from the ashes, soar into the sky, and watch over us from above.

Track 10: won't you celebrate with me
Lucille Clifton

won't you celebrate with me
what i have shaped into
a kind of life? i had no model.
born in babylon
both nonwhite and woman
what did i see to be except myself?
i made it up
here on this bridge between
starshine and clay,
my one hand holding tight
my other hand; come celebrate
with me that everyday
something has tried to kill me
and has failed.

❉ ❉ ❉ ❉

Outro: Although this poem showcases the difficulty of being Black in America, it also celebrates the strength and perseverance of African Americans. Within a historical context, "won't you celebrate with me" addresses the dangers of being a Black person—in this case, the Black woman—in the United States. And yet, they are still alive. This poem boldly looks back, honoring ancestors, and leaps forward into the future. The celebration is in the living when history, politics, and circumstances said, *You should not make it.*

Track 11: Douen
Lauren K. Alleyne

I.

Baby never slipped
    fully into his name.

Never had the chill of holy
    water kiss his scalp—make him

bawl down the church.
    Never survive but a few

months after his mother
    crooned *Yes, douxdoux!*

Hello, choonkchoonks!
    into his brand-new ear—

still brown at the tips,
    still unused to sound

but always turning
  towards it. Never hear

de bacchanal that buss
  out his mother's throat

when she peeped into the crib
  that was squatting quiet-quiet

in the bedroom corner
  like the prophecy of a coffin

and reach down her hand
  to touch his chest—still-

warm, echoless. Her scream
  couldn't quite wake the dead,

but the milk-soaked sound of it
  catch him like a rope round the ankles—

Come back, nah douxdoux.
Come back. Come back.

II.

It not easy to enter this world,
    but it even harder to leave it:

the body is a stubborn grief,
    will hold even the shadowed

memory of itself and call it survival.

III.

They say Douen have no face,
    only mouth—that hollow, hungry

port with its traffic of things
    that go in one way and come out

another, if at all. Or leave
    and never come back the same.

Think bread. Think breath.

IV.

And just like that, he here:
    a presence: here: a present

unconjugatable tense: here:
    a between-thing: here: a dusking

with no nightfall: here: a dawn
    that will never break: here: he

a frayed straw hat slumped
    on an infant's idea of a head:

here: he a name that summons
    nothing: here: he a thin longing

only a child's ear can catch:
    here: *can you hear?*

V.

A forest is a here place.

VI.

They say you know a Douen
   by the wrongness of its feet—

the impossible, unholy turn of them
   —knees overseeing the heels,

toes seeking shelter under calves—
   but baby never knew *walk* or *run*,

never tottered into the real-life
   language of legs, so he invent them:

a grammar to hold: here:
   the contradictory anatomy of grief:

Come. Back. Come. Back.
   Come. Back. Come. Back.

꙼ ꙼ ꙼ ꙼

Outro: The Douen is a mythological creature in folklore from Trinidad and Tobago. It's a frightening creature with strange eyes, backward feet, and a floppy hat that hides its facelessness. The creature likes to lure children into the woods, where they become lost. This poem thinks about the different meanings of being lost within the context of grief, how sometimes one can become lost, and the way back seems impossible.

Vol. 2: Gawd

If we do not now dare everything, the fulfillment of that prophecy, re-created from the Bible in song by a slave, is upon us: God gave Noah the rainbow sign, No more water, the fire next time!

—James Baldwin

Track 1: Genesis

Etheridge Knight

the skin
of my poems
May be green, yes,
and sometimes
wrinkled
or worn

the snake shape
of my song
may cause
the heel
of Adam & Eve
to bleed . . .

split my skin
with the rock
of love old
as the rock
of Moses

my poems

love you

✻ ✻ ✻ ✻

Outro: There are obvious biblical references scattered throughout
this poem, but the poem seems to be saying that (though green and
new) the poem carries magic. The poem loves you. The poem loves
you in a giving way. The way the rock gave Moses water, after he
struck it, in the Bible. The reference to the snakelike quality to the
poem clearly points out that this poem also may be thinking of sin.

Track 2: Exodus

Jamar J. Perry

I.

Lord, please deliver me
cause Hurting me
is all I seem to do

I was thirty-two when I realized this.

Mama loves you and she
            needs you to forgive her.

                            Is that all you can say?
                            we only speak
                            over the phone.

I didn't mean to.
I was a young mother.
I wanted to make men out of y'all, you and your three brothers.

The words drop from steel, ferocious, lips as lies,
covered in sweet chocolates, strawberries, and mint.
From the age of twelve, I knew, but you didn't.

II.

I remember, I am four, already too tall for my age.

He beat me, mercilessly
because I peed the bed like rivers,
my tears matching the lifeforce
that trickled from me like waterfalls: no escape, but falling
   nonetheless
      Because you abandoned me.

I am twelve now, my arm broken,
as broken as my soul is.
I become quiet, no longer able to speak up for myself,
not to you or him,
or the children who bully me to show
that they are superior to me in every way.
      And they were.

Mama took me to the doctor,
but he made me go back to that hell.

My arm broken, my life broken, my soul
    B r o k e n
Half of my heart gone with you not being able to fill
the other side
    Because you neglected me

III.

I am now fifteen, my shoulder broken this time.
I did it to make men out of you and your brothers.
No showers, eating on dirty floors, the regular beatings,
    no friends.
        I can't wait to leave this house, I would say
If you want to leave, you can always go to church, you'd say.

    But you never went.

The church was not my salvation, either.
It was filled with hypocrisies, lies leaving their lips
like blood fills open, wounded mouths,
like caverns that would swallow me whole when I protested.

IV.

I'm seventeen now,
finally have a job so that I can save enough to leave your home,
to leave your hatred.

To live in my house, you need to pay me rent, you'd say.
I barely graduated, because you'd take from me
when you were supposed to give, and give,
and give,
until you couldn't anymore.
But all you did was take.
Because you abused me.

I struggled after leaving your cold embrace,
no longer knowing what love meant
because love was nowhere in you.
Relationships, struggled
Love, nonexistent
Friendships, strained
Arguments, a common *me* pastime
Depression, visited upon me like demons.

That river of tears is now an expansive sea,
one of possibilities, travels, transitions,
of vastness.

I embrace all of the trials and tribulations to come on my
journey,
    because love of self exists within, outside, and *through*
    them.

I refuse to let my Genesis be my Exodus.

❧ ❧ ❧ ❧

Outro: Generational trauma happens when the stress/trauma
of one generation is passed to the next. This poem investigates
the impact of generational trauma in the Black community. The
author of this poem says, *The speaker in the poem is claiming their
history and learning to set healthy boundaries while remembering the
difficulties of childhood.* Often, setting these boundaries is the first
step in healing. The poem is divided into sections, which helps
propel the narrative arc of the speaker.

Track 3: Soup-her-stitions

Jeanine Jones

As the Wonder boy sings how very superstitious it is

Auntie spits on brooms that hit her feet

Spitting off the luck of going to jail or hell

warns all the nieces and nephews to avoid stepping on cracks,

Hand itchin' for money

Don't put your purse on the floor girl

low money to no money is the result

Read your Bible every day

                        cuss out God when you mad

Maybe he'll hear you

Counting rosary beads, hanging on to the Hail Marys of

   Catholicism

and her superstitions

Soup-her-stitions ~~lived~~ feared by

Intel of religion,

Believed in, couldn't live by though

Mass and ashes on forehead

Cigarette between lips

Voo-doing the lucky John between her hips

Pink Champale in glass, She sips

Preach'n, not practicing

~~Putting~~ Teaching fear in all the nieces and nephews with her

Soup-her-stitions

Warning us all to fear nobody

Stirring us into the soup of her beliefs

Worshipped, loved and feared, conjuring spells

She laughs

oo-ya

upid-sta

other-ma uckers-fa

e-ba eeve-la

at-wha ever-ya

I-ya

ay-sa

❊ ❊ ❊ ❊

Outro: The author of this poem says, *The inspiration for "Soup-her-stitions" comes from years of tales told by the storytellers, the griots known as aunts and uncles who told the same stories to generations of the family, instilling beliefs and traditions in younger family members based on myths and superstitions.* Some traditions were based on Catholicism, which was not the norm for Black families. The poet adds, *That practice [Catholicism] was learned as my grandmother, who worked in the rectory doing* *housework, and my grandfather, who worked in a steel mill in addition to many other jobs, struggled to put their ten children through Catholic school.*

Track 4: Runaway

Ryan Douglass

my father was a kid, cut on barbed-wire fence—
his son a cratered knuckle, air filling up a blister.
our water is hard-tinged,
our truth exchanged for fake compliments.
we speak of fear and power
disparate passengers on transit.

the gospel speaks through me less
sunday's best than fallen angel disrobing.
off comes my skin like no one is in it—
when he lifted my frame one-handed from the crib
the ancestors saw what he did.

little saplings and lashings and left-leaning lids.
my sister sent a succulent i tossed upon cleaning.
how revenge can be a dream, or a punch line, or a grid.
soon as i get the means, i am out of this country
to drink like an orphaned kid.
i watched a spot behind my eyelids

and found a burst of color,
a music of joyful remembrance.

i am my mother's son, and a broken lung,
ill, as prey that would sooner
stand still when a serpent stalks its way.
the circle of life is like glass eyes
behind open windows witnessing strange abuses.
i know a compassion that folds its form into the attic
and feels as doomed, as useless.

i will be alone, resigned and lonely
as the seafarer rows.
and ask i will of the beckoning flood
to forgive the blood on my cuffs.
i love my family dearly
and miss them not nearly enough.

⚹ ⚹ ⚹ ⚹

Outro: This poem looks at Black familial relations and intergenerational trauma in a nuanced way. The poem respects the strength of love that exists in these bonds but also how those bonds change over time. It's a complex dance. The speaker addresses the alienation that has occurred from their family as they've grown up, how certain relationships feel unresolved, and how they've made peace with solitude.

Track 5: The Lynching

Claude McKay

His spirit in smoke ascended to high heaven.
His father, by the cruelest way of pain,
Had bidden him to his bosom once again;
The awful sin remained still unforgiven.
All night a bright and solitary star
(Perchance the one that ever guided him,
Yet gave him up at last to Fate's wild whim)
Hung pitifully o'er the swinging char.
Day dawned, and soon the mixed crowds came to view
The ghastly body swaying in the sun:
The women thronged to look, but never a one
Showed sorrow in her eyes of steely blue;
And little lads, lynchers that were to be,
Danced round the dreadful thing in fiendish glee.

❧ ❧ ❧ ❧

Outro: From 1880 to 1968, there were over 4,600 recorded lynchings
in the United States. The practice was often seen as an event in
the South that white people would attend and watch. This poem

describes—in gruesome detail—the reality of these hateful events. In saying that the lynching mob "danced round the dreadful thing in fiendish glee," the poet characterizes the devilish nature of racism and those who acted on it in the American South. It also points out the inhumanity in the observer.

Track 6: A Hymn to the Evening
Phillis Wheatley

Soon as the sun forsook the eastern main
The pealing thunder shook the heav'nly plain;
Majestic grandeur! From the zephyr's wing,
Exhales the incense of the blooming spring.
Soft purl the streams, the birds renew their notes,
And through the air their mingled music floats.

Through all the heav'ns what beauteous dies are spread!
But the west glories in the deepest red:
So may our breasts with ev'ry virtue glow,
The living temples of our God below!

Fill'd with the praise of him who gives the light,
And draws the sable curtains of the night,
Let placid slumbers sooth each weary mind,
At morn to wake more heav'nly, more refin'd;
So shall the labours of the day begin
More pure, more guarded from the snares of sin.

Night's leaden sceptre seals my drowsy eyes,
Then cease, my song, till fair *Aurora* rise.

❧ ❧ ❧ ❧

Outro: Nature is often seen as magnificent in poetry and song. This poem exalts the beauty of an evening sunset. The speaker in this poem has a deep appreciation for the miracles on earth. The poem is also in form with a distinct rhyme scheme, three stanzas, and a final rhyming couplet. The form adds to the lyrical quality of the piece.

Track 7: Five in One
Ama Asantewa Diaka

Because he was the first to survive not dying
my great-great-great-grandfather was raised like a king

how well acquainted with pain are you
if all the prayers in your throat
do not keep your first four babies alive
before their fourth week?

& so when the fifth one survives a month
You name him he whose breath still remains
You name him he who the ancestors prayed here
You name him the water that doused the fire blue
the cry that cracks open things until what belongs is returned
the seed that arrived in time for man to make linen out of sweat
You name him a good good thing

His black eyes look back at you as if to say:
There is awe in knowing that I have not died yet

When he survives more months than your fingers can count
You sing a potion into his bones:

Thumbs greener than the Garden of Eden
A mind sharp enough to slice through metal
An orb of grace
A tongue that assumes the weight of a village

For he is the one whose breath still remains
King—others returned to the earth so you could stand firm in it

⚘ ⚘ ⚘ ⚘

Outro: This poem reads like a psalm for life and gratitude. The survival of the child in this poem elevates them, promotes them to an important figure in the community—a miracle that has been touched by some god, a King. The narrative arc and tone of the poem also adds to the implications that what is happening here is in some way divine, especially with the passing of so many children before.

Track 8: Other World: A Veneration

Faylita Hicks

\/\/

I am:
  Other world.
    Gxrl gone mad.
    Exodus evolved.
    Hoodoo womxn.
  Marassa; the middle path.
  Part crown, part root.

\/\/

I am: The Mirror; the moon; mimicking the dove; swallowing.

\/\/

  I am: Oshun; honey glaze; golden; sweet waters; divine.
  I am: Yemayá; stitched into mermaid's hair or the sun: Dani,
    salt-heavy with moan.

I am: Erzulie; mounting love like a blush on the cheek.

I am: Ogun; hammer and hail; knocking against the eve
of the aeon.

I am: Of and in and from Laveau's elixir dream.

I am: Obatala; Mountains, like me, climb and fall, roll and
reach; palm wine and critique.

I am: Oyá; what no man will ever be able to wrap his tongue
around; a sound

that piston rings in and out of fashion. *I hear.*

I am: Shango; a cut above and below; coming.

I am: Here. *Far away from here.*

With Legba, walking Elegua

where hope is still real and curls into light;

ears cupped like hands around our secrets.

I am: The face of the drum, the houngan calling on me;
Doctor of the verve.

\/\/

I am: Without fear or without fear of.

I am: Release and reinstate.

I am: The satiate; the hunger abate.

I is: A dream remixed and reworked.

I be: The coffee; the gleaned bean; the gleam.

Olodumare is in me.

I am: Otherworld. The Other Gxrl.

Without: I am. (Within).

❧ ❧ ❧ ❧

Outro: The poet says, *The earliest version of this poem was written in late 2010, shortly after the death of my fiancé in April and my arrest for a bounced check to a grocery store a month later in May.* The speaker in the poem, in a way, feels powerless. The poet goes on to say, *In the months that followed, I went again and again to the river that ran just outside my apartment complex—the Guadalupe. There, I began reconnecting with my ancestors' teachings and starting the healing process. The wisdom of the Orishas trickled down to me over the next several years, arriving at prescient moments. I learned that I was not alone in this body; I am, at a cellular level, filled with all the experiences of every person in my lineage. I began to understand that liberation was about more than living outside of the carceral state and its emphasis on individuality; it was about embracing the interconnectedness inherent in the human experience and eroding the borders placed on our imaginations and hearts.*

Track 9: 20/20

Simone Liggins

I have two eyes—one Black, one White,
grown and developed by two torn sides
for 32 springs and autumns.
Their perceptions merge and split,
searching for the view of healing truth
in this ever-wounded land. What do you have to tell me
about these two bold hues? They sift through
the sagging grey veil that bears the power of malicious
    segregation,
still trapped in a bad romance burning for the last 400 years.
How sad it is to consider yourself lucky to be called your
    original American brand
only twice to your face
while trying to breathe through the rest that sound
as if in desperate need of education.
Like the time that sweet old granny asked—in front of her
    granddaughter—
if I knew that Black people usually named their children
too "uniquely."

Or when an old friend's sister mistook me for the Venezuelan
  housemaid.
Or when a hip-out geometry teacher pulled me aside,
felt the need to explain that saying any version of "nigger"
  was wrong
because her own access was denied and that I'd probably want
to kill any white person showing their privilege.
Talk about coming to terms with one's destiny.
Cue every cackle, accepting my role as Teacher and Ambassador
between bomb-sheltered realities is one fuck of a mean feat.
Dare to ask me questions?
Dare to hear my answers.
I silently snicker as my eyes watch yours
and read your mind as free words shred it
a newly perceived vision: That language is my birthright;
I'm not an angry Black woman, only exasperated;
I'll love whoever I want and will gladly smile in your face
  with them on my arm.
Try to comprehend that which you'll only comprehend
with just the right dosage of enlightenment.
Hold new hope, my pupil. Show me your teeth.
Bite my apple, if you dare.

❊ ❊ ❊ ❊

Outro: This poem showcases a litany of moments in the Black experience, but the apple reference located in the final line brings forth the image of Adam and Eve. The apple in this narrative poem could be seen as the knowledge of the duality and difficulty of the Black experience that outsiders do not understand.

Track 10: Paper Mills
Antwan Eady

It came without warning
This snow in the South
When it fell from the skies
Having never lived in the clouds

Momma calls it
the sick
'Cause it makes Gramma cough

Papa calls it
Bittersweet
The way it makes ends meet

Auntie calls it
a shame
Since *it wasn't always this way*

But me
I call it
The Snow

'Cause how could I look
My baby brother in his eyes . . .
and tell him *Death*

Just fell from heaven

❉ ❉ ❉ ❉

Outro: Inspired by the world we live in, "Paper Mills" sheds a light on environmental injustices predominantly Black communities and low-income communities face today and how these communities are disproportionately affected by the placement of potentially toxic facilities in our neighborhoods. The poet says, *These facilities may include, but are not limited to, coal-fired power plants, hazardous waste facilities, and paper mills, to name a few. The release of certain chemicals can endanger air quality, water quality, the soil we grow our vegetables in, and more, leading to health consequences such as birth defects and cancer.* Today, predominantly Black communities and low-income communities throughout the United States remain threatened.

Track 11: Hottentot Girl Summer
Ibi Zoboi

(for Lucille Clifton's "homage to my hips")

This
is not
a BBL—
More like a
divine African
throne, Venus
seated high, tall
shelf table top booty
A place for the
world to rest its
weary feet when
I carry it on
my back even
as they watch me
drop it like it's hot
girl summer so thick
with it Woke up like
this Born like this is not
a BBL More like
DNA in these
tight ass
genes

❉ ❉ ❉ ❉

Outro: This poem reclaims Black women's bodies. It celebrates their power, strength, and endurance throughout the centuries. This poem offers no apology—only pride. It is a timely nod to Clifton's poem "homage to my hips," once again leaning into the idea that the bodies of Black women do not have to fit into anyone's box.

# Vol. 3: Haunting Water

Don't threaten me with love, baby. Let's just
go walking in the rain.
—Billie Holiday

Track 1: *Wrath of Scaled Gods*

Mahogany L. Browne

I want to tell you a story
about a fin torn dolphin
black slick oil mammal
who cut beneath the ocean near
Captiva an island ready town
with a mouth full of rickety floorboards
It was so familiar
like the time the black Cadillac or Cutlass
(or was it even black?)
swerved the streets of West Oakland
pummeled potholes
and
broken noise beaming between
each shock absorption
wheez a heavy-wombed being
searching for something bright enuff to snuff
Just in time to find us three teenagers w/ too much smile
& not enough smoke
on our lips

Brakes pump and doors swing open—
a monster returning to clean its plate of stubborn morsels
Twenty-five years later
And this memory swims obtrusively
through my vision of blk dolphins
swimming by the Fish House every January morning
I sit on the deck of this house named after a sea of scaled gods
A New Yorker with a sweet tooth for salt water
named this stilted dreamscape along the listless
cove of Captiva, Florida
Here we are required to converse deeply with our muse
rather than small talk with mortals
I swoon like I've never been nowhere before
Until you grab
the five-point pulsing star fruit
from the tree stout and bursting
out the wet earth of your front yard
maybe you haven't ever really lived
Or maybe you don't know what to call survival
when your blood still Brazilian waves at the sight
of Black doors flashing under hot lights
ready to swing open and pour cement
on anything
with a pulse throbbing
to feed the emptying knot growing

I peer over my coffee cup
a Keurig mess disguised
as good enough and wait
for the commute of my new mammal friend
blk fin returns each morning
tear marked and followed
closely by a crew of smaller fins
She swims by and I sing Good Morning
Her wet ripped glistens in reply
O stolen dolphin meat by a greedy fork or gang
We are so much alike
I close my mouth upturn my face to the sun completely
Let the heat kiss me the way I've wanted love all my life
O torn fin friend, I hum
We are reflective discs of Black wonder:
shredded, stained and still gliding against the trembling
    currents
Refusing to sink

⚹ ⚹ ⚹ ⚹

Outro: Memory, myth, and magic mingle in this poem, which highlights how our upbringings inform how we perceive the world. The poem also tells a story within a story. It is a narrative that respects the concrete jungle, nature, animals, and childhood equally—because they all have the tenacity to survive.

Track 2: Portrait of a Daughter
Donald Vincent (aka Mr. Hip)

The world is your canvas. Don't forget
to stroke it with the blues of your ancestors,

those souls full of muddy waters, collards,
hot combs and iron cast skillets. Are your

dreams made of butterfly barrettes
                and prancy pirouettes?

It's not that Jesus didn't walk on water,
he danced—a double-dutch across currents.

Every dip a sacrament. Here
bath time is a holy ritual. Hear

            the sacred waves that cleanse.

❊ ❊ ❊ ❊

Outro: The poet says, *While my five-month-old daughter is the muse for this poem, these words were inspired by all of the Black women in my life. This poem reflects on being present and in the moment, whether it is a carefree afternoon on the playground, everyday maintenance, or a diligent day at the dance studio.* The history of dance and its ancestral ties run deep within African American culture and will always serve as holy moments in the innocent lives of Black women worldwide.

Track 3: Moon Wants in on the Groove
DeeSoul Carson

In the mid-2030s, every U.S. coast will experience rapidly increasing high-tide floods, when a lunar cycle will amplify rising sea levels caused by climate change. —NASA

NASA says by 2030, the moon will be doing the Wobble, & I don't know shit about science, except that it says we're gonna get ourselves killed, but I know a thing or two about the moon, how it pulls up & brings all the water. I know when water comes to coast, it comes looking for blood & finds Black folk instead. I know if I was more than 20ft from shore, I'd be a goner. I know somewhere beneath the waves, I've got family too familiar with water weight, but Moon ain't really tryna hear that shit. Moon just wanna skate & electric slide like them old heads. Moon wanna get down & get on up, wanna two-step & diddy bop, want someone to believe them when they say *The world is ending tomorrow, baby, so we might as well dance.* Moon wanna roll bounce, rock skate, wanna glide knife-smooth, wanna hollywood swing like they daddy. Moon want Auntie's 7UP cake. Want granny's gumbo.

Wanna come home to mama's two-day-old spaghetti in the Country Crock container, wanna hear mama fuss at them to go wash the outside off. Moon wanna hear uncle's drunk, raspy laugh when mama says he ain't no good, wanna hear grandpa tell them to stop all that arguing. Moon want a warm dark, a summer breeze, a dog to bark all through the night. Moon wanna tell all they people they love them & want all they people to say it back. Say it loud. Say it so proud the water stands still.

❊　❊　❊　❊

Outro: The poet offers, *Part of this poem's structure was inspired by reading Karisma Price's "My Phone Autocorrects 'Nigga' to 'Night'" in the June 2020 issue of* Poetry *magazine. When writing this poem considering the NASA article, I wondered what it would mean for the moon and its wobble/dance, despite its pending havoc, to stand in for those I love, my brothers and sisters and cousins.*

Track 4: This Is Not a Small Voice

Sonia Sanchez

This is not a small voice
you hear   this is a large
voice coming out of these cities.
This is the voice of LaTanya.
Kadesha. Shaniqua. This
is the voice of Antoine.
Darryl. Shaquille.
Running over waters
navigating the hallways
of our schools spilling out
on the corners of our cities and
no epitaphs spill out of their river
mouths.

This is not a small love
you hear   this is a large
love, a passion for kissing learning
on its face.
This is a love that crowns the feet

with hands
that nourishes, conceives, feels the
water sails mends the children,
folds them inside our history
where they
toast more than the flesh
where they suck the bones of the
alphabet
and spit out closed vowels.
This is a love colored with iron
and lace.
This is a love initialed Black
Genius.
This is not a small voice
you hear.

⚹ ⚹ ⚹ ⚹

Outro: Voices are important. They can yell, shout, scream, cry, and talk. The voices and experiences of Black people are vast. This poem utilizes the image of water to show the vastness of the Black experience and Black culture. Black culture, just like water, seeps into many aspects of society.

Track 5: Loophole of Retreat
Joy Priest

Every Black girl needs a loophole
in the fabric of reality. A special room
where her world is what she imagines,

a place to slip inside, a secret kept
with oneself, a portal out of captivity.
Harriet Jacobs waited in the garret

of her grandmother's house for seven
years to escape to freedom. With
only the world she could imagine

to occupy her mind, with only
muffled voices and mice for company.
Denver found an emerald room

of boxwood bushes, where she hid
the scent of wild veronica and herself
from *the hurt world*, from fear and grief: —

What will be your special place? Dark
hideaway? Hidden room of trees?
What kind of world will you imagine
in your Black girl portal, hiding free?

꙰ ꙰ ꙰ ꙰

Outro: This villanelle enacts the thing it describes: a loophole.
"Loophole of Retreat" is a phrase Harriet Jacobs uses in her slave
narrative *Incidents in the Life of a Slave Girl*, and Denver is a character
in *Beloved* by Toni Morrison—the surviving daughter of Sethe. It's
an interactive poem: The final stanza is a prompt. A villanelle is a
poem that has five three-line stanzas and a final four-line stanza.

Track 6: The Southern Mermaid
Amber McBride

Grandpa, tell me that story—
the one where the Mississippi
grew legs, stepped over its banks
and dug ten toes into the mossy soil.

Remind me how the river
can't be trusted, how it once tried to stick a snake
down your throat, but Grandma woke just in time—
   slurped the flood down as easy as sweet tea.

Tell me about the skin
tattooed with snakes, golden bracelets
raining down slimy arms
with bones made of cane sugar,
tobacco leaves, cotton fluff and silver needles.

Tell me again, Grandpa,
how you, Grandma and me
were all baptized in a filthy southern lake,
surrounded by bloated fish.

The mermaid didn't get us,
but the rocks left scars, like snake bites
on the bottoms of our feet.

⚹ ⚹ ⚹ ⚹

Outro: In African culture, Mami Wata is a water spirit who was feared but fair. This poem imagines a different kind of mermaid in the Mississippi River. One that is not written in African or African American culture. A more mischievous mermaid—a mermaid who could cause harm. Growing up in central Virginia, I was often told tales about a river mermaid who could sometimes walk on land. I don't know if I was afraid of her, but I did not go by the river at night.

Track 7: Untitled

James Baldwin

Lord,

> when you send the rain
> think about it, please,
> a little?

Do

> not get carried away
> by the sound of falling water,
> the marvelous light
> on the falling water.

I

> am beneath that water.
> It falls with great force
> and the light

Blinds

> me to the light.

❦ ❦ ❦ ❦

Outro: This compact poem packs a punch! It directly addresses
the Lord, asking him to hold off on the rain as it is something that

burdens the speaker. There is a clear distance between the Lord and the speaker, who is under the water, trapped. The image of water often represents cleansing and baptism, but the speaker seems to be stuck in this state, which begs the question, How are we redeemed?

Track 8: The Little Black Boy Finds Some Shade

Tariq Thompson

an erasure of Louise Glück's 2020 Nobel Lecture

Little Black

Boy

a village

singing,

How

history

was

a

grave.

this seemed

natural myths filled

with

invisible

dead, but he was alive,

speaking

longing

little black boy

little black boy

feeling

revenge   in the

perfect world

he is   a

sudden surfeit of

hope

heartbreak   righteous

anger the little black boy

is a child.

you and I

a   kind

of   prec   ious

power

What happens to

the living

?

We   a fact

we

a

safe place

I am   talking   about

trust

That

sudden

future

* * * *

Outro: When approaching writing this poem the author says, *I chose to erase Louise Glück's 2020 Nobel Lecture in which she invokes the image of "The Little Black Boy," because, when first reading it, I remember thinking: "He must be lonely. He must be tired of being used." I chose to lead with care rather than violence (in Solmaz Sharif's words, "I do not wish to replicate state control or participate in obliteration's etymology"). I sought to excavate language that recognized him as a complex, imperfect human being; language that could witness him fully; language that could, finally, give him some company. After all, I am a Black boy, too.*

Track 9: Follow the Drinking Gourd
Author Unknown (American Folk Song)

Follow the drinking gourd! Follow the drinking gourd.

For the old man is waiting to carry you to freedom

Follow the drinking gourd.

When the sun goes back and the first quail calls

Follow the drinking gourd

The old man is a-waitin' to carry you to freedom

Follow the drinking gourd

Follow the drinking gourd! Follow the drinking gourd.

For the old man is waiting to carry you to freedom

Follow the drinking gourd.

The river bed makes a mighty fine road,

Dead trees to show you the way

And it's left foot, peg foot, traveling on

Follow the drinking gourd

Follow the drinking gourd! Follow the drinking gourd.

For the old man is waiting to carry you to freedom

Follow the drinking gourd.

The river ends between two hills

Follow the drinking gourd

There's another river on the other side

Follow the drinking gourd

Follow the drinking gourd! Follow the drinking gourd.

For the old man is waiting to carry you to freedom

Follow the drinking gourd.

I thought I heard the angels say

Follow the drinking gourd

The stars in the heavens gonna show you the way

Follow the drinking gourd

Follow the drinking gourd! Follow the drinking gourd.

For the old man is waiting to carry you to freedom

Follow the drinking gourd.

Follow the drinking gourd! Follow the drinking gourd.

For the old man is waiting to carry you to freedom

Follow the drinking gourd.

Follow the drinkin' gourd.

❧ ❧ ❧ ❧

Outro: The direct origin of this song is unknown, but it is a direct reference to the Big Dipper. The song was sung to offer secret directions for enslaved people to find their way to free states and Canada on the Underground Railroad. The song has continued to have great importance to this day. It is a symbol of strength and ingenuity during difficult times and a reminder of what our Black ancestors endured.

Track 10: Middle Passage: Day One

Kwame Alexander

The Wonderfuls
bring misery
and destruction to those
who do not look like them.

Their eyes covet the whole earth
and they see us as shadows
to step on.

They do not care
of our celestial origins,
that we descended
from the Great Good above.
They do not respect
our traditions
our heroic past
the power of women
the wisdom of elders
and spiders
the joy of peace.

They ignore the life-giving palm fruit
for its slippery, sweet profits
and cannot see even a glimmer of gold
for the riches it yields.

They do not care about
honoring the stars or
the magnificent sky
that houses them,
only that they can use it
to guide them toward
plunder.

The mighty river
that births us, to them
is a speedy path
to our destruction.

This place
is not a castle
of anything good.
It is a dungeon
empty of heart
and these alien people
with their wolfish logic
and wicked impulses

will eat at our flesh
until the blood of Asante dries,
and our steady beat is no more.
That is their way.

Since I came here
with child
eight months ago
I have counted
one hundred
and twelve
children
and women
taken from this damp, dark cell
never to return,
and each day
I kneel down
and say a prayer
to Bona, the Great One
that breathes mountains,
that my first child,
my beautiful little boy
who was unborn
days ago
right where you lay,
is near a star

in the sky
reunited
with all
that is good.

✻ ✻ ✻ ✻

Outro: This persona poem is told from the perspective of a woman who is being held before enduring the Middle Passage. The duality of this poem is highlighted in how life, death, hope, and faith are all seen conversing with each other on the page. It also comments on the duality of water—how it both offers life and carries Black bodies into bondage.

Track 11: New Curriculum on Water

Taylor Byas

If I let science tell me everything, I'd be
lost. Sometimes, there can be more than one

reason, I mean sometimes, two things
can be true. I mean, the moon ain't

the only thing tugging the tides, pulling
waves from the shore. I've passed

all of my science classes and water remains
a mystery because they don't teach it

right. Say it got three states but there are
four, or more—*solid, liquid, gas, whisper,*

killer, healer—I have been on an empty beach
and listened intently to the crash

of an ancestor's voice, an old song
from the deep. I have sunk into

the cradle of a lawn chair, watched
a couple scatter as their toddler

chased the retreating foam. I've warmed
a cup of salt water and gargled it,

let it soothe an irritated throat. Sometimes,
a thing is so many things, we try to name it

one. Sometimes, the pressure of water
is too much for its container.

⋇ ⋇ ⋇ ⋇

Outro: This poem considers the mystical and supernatural quality of water, how it has so many uses and purposes, is simultaneously dangerous and restorative. Additionally, water is of significant historical importance in Black history, serving as a symbol of tragedy in some instances, and a beacon of hope in others.

Vol. 4: Magickal

No, I do not weep at the world—I am too
busy sharpening my oyster knife.
—Zora Neale Hurston

Track 1: Mumble the Magic Words

Jabari Asim

Come, claim your wings.
Lift your life above the earth,
return to the land of your father's birth.

Come, unbend your back.
Let us fade together in a trick of light.
Let us gather stars and ride the night,
never forgetting those who've forgotten
beneath the lash and sting of cotton.

kum kunka yali,
kum . . . tambe!
buba yali
buba tambe

Mumble the magic words.
Seize the sky as soaring birds.

✶ ✶ ✶ ✶

Outro: The author says, *This poem is part of a series inspired by tales of our enslaved ancestors, who solved the riddle of flight by unlocking their tongues and taking wing, all the way home to Africa.* The poem conjures a spell and a way home to freedom. *It also empowers us and our ancestors.*

Track 2: A Fable
Etheridge Knight

Once upon a today and yesterday and nevermore there were
7 men and women all locked / up in prison cells. Now these
7 men and women were innocent of any crimes; they were
in prison because their skins were black. Day after day, the
prisoners paced their cells, pining for their freedom. And the
non-black jailers would laugh at the prisoners and beat them
with sticks and throw their food on the floor. Finally, prisoner
#1 said, "I will educate myself and emulate the non-colored
people. That is the way to freedom—c'mon, you guys, and
follow me." "Hell, no," said prisoner #2. "The *only* way to
get free is to pray to my god and he will deliver you like he
delivered Daniel from the lion's den, so unite and follow me."
"Bullshit," said prisoner #3. "The *only* way / out is thru this
tunnel i've been quietly digging, so c'mon, and follow me."
"Uh-uh," said prisoner #4, "that's too risky. The only right /
way is to follow all the rules and don't make the non-colored
people angry, so c'mon brothers and sisters and unite behind
me." "Fuck you!" said prisoner #5, "The *only* way / out is to
shoot our way out, if all of you get / together behind me."

"No," said prisoner #6, "all of you are incorrect; you have not analyzed the political situation by my scientific method and historical meemeejeebee. All we have to do is wait long enough and the bars will bend from their own inner rot. That is the *only* way." "Are all of you crazy," cried prisoner #7. "I'll get out by myself, by ratting on the rest of you to the non-colored people. That is the way, that is the *only* way!" "No-no," they / all cried, "come and follow me. I have the / way, the only way to freedom." And so they argued, and to this day they are still arguing; and to this day they are still in their prison cells, their stomachs / trembling with fear.

⁂ ⁂ ⁂ ⁂

Outro: "A Fable" approaches the idea of how mass incarceration disproportionately affects people of color. It is set up as a fable and explains the circumstances of seven individuals. The case is shown as if an omniscient narrator is looking down at the situation and clicking his tongue at the injustice. This poem works to show the complexity of each of the seven individuals but also, as many folktales do, illustrates how they all meet the same fate because of the color of their skin. Like a record on repeat, this same story is playing out in prisons across America because of ongoing racism.

Track 3: Anansi's Bop
Rodrick Minor

Spidering beneath the moonlight
At the hour of fire & mutiny
Anansi's eyes, bulbous and bright
like lanterns leading Black boys home
Before bullets & gunmetal police
the status quo of our whereabouts

What a cobweb life we live?

All blueblack, like the spider
Sprinting toward the cold
Gaze of his predator's eyes
Piercing the silence at a traffic stop
as the cop's eyes are full of venom
Anansi's arms cloak us Black boys
Watching over our celestial bodies
Before the night erases us into relics

What a cobweb life we weave?

Crawling into the havens after dawn
　　Anansi protects
Anansi protects the boys protects the boys the boys

Anansi　　**Anansi**
BLACK　　**Anansi** boysboys **Anansi**
Anansi boysboys **Anansi**　　boys
boys　　**Anansi**
Anansi　　**BLACK**
Anansi　　**BLACK Anansi** boysboys **Anansi Anansi**
BOYS boys
Anansi

Anansi　　**Anansi Anansi** boysboys **Anansi**　　**Anansi**
boysboys **Anansi**
boys　　boys
Anansi　　**Anansi**

What a cobweb life we celebrate?

⋇　⋇　⋇　⋇

Outro: The poet says, *"Anansi's Bop" is a political love poem in response to the police brutality against Black lives, especially Black boys.* Regarding the form of the poem, the poet adds, *The bop is a poetic form invented by Afaa Michael Weaver, consisting of three stanzas and* *a repeated line expanding a poetic dilemma, the dilemma in this case being the ongoing threat of living as Black boys, with Anansi being a refuge and light.* This poem is a constant discourse of navigating the intersections of survival, joy, and love of Black life, Black boys.

Track 4: Enough Room
Taylor Byas

—why the Sun and the Moon live in the sky

And what to tell a man
whose job is to be sure of his hands

and their measurements? Before the Sun
was a nosy eye he was a carpenter, marking

everything by the black teeth of his
measuring tape. Built a house for him and his

wife while she hollered over the weep
of his machines, the saw and sander too hot

from his touch. *Make enough room for guests*,
said the Moon. *Enough room, enough room.*

And the Sun measured only for two
and a few more, the front door barely wide

enough for him and the Moon to pass through
at once. When the house was done, the Sun's

old friend Water stopped by, the eye
of his storm a pocket for all his creatures.

And when he stepped inside he spread,
flooded the bedrooms, kitchen,

basement, wasted no time lifting everything
from its place. Left no space for the Sun

and the Moon, and soon they had
to flee to the dry of the clouds. In the sky,

the Sun began again on a new home,
the yellow of his measuring tape as bright

as the smile his wife wouldn't give
him. While he worked, he mumbled, *Enough*

room, enough room. The Moon shook
her head in silence, and looked on.

❋ ❋ ❋ ❋

Outro: Folklore is filled with creation stories—how the tiger got his stripes, why the giraffe has a long neck. This poem explains why the Sun and the Moon are in the sky. The personification of the Sun and Moon works in the tradition of folklore, where nature is an active character in creation.

Track 5: (un)chained
Erica Martin

go ahead—

trap our bodies

in shackles
behind bars

build your prisons on the grounds
where our ancestors lie
free

beneath the earth
unmarked

go ahead—

move us from plantations
to penal farms

by way of the
new old laws

as if you could lock up

                                        our will to survive

✴ ✴ ✴ ✴

Outro: This poem speaks to the shared history of African Americans.
It is a fiery poem about the history of injustices African Americans
have faced. It speaks on the Black experience and the different types
of prisons Black Americans find themselves in.

Track 6: Ink & Thunderstorms
Amber McBride

cracked it (the fable)
about Black bodies thrown out
or jumping ship to sea

their shadows knitting & mixing
with waves and thunderclaps
crafting salty wings

found it (inked it out)
recovered each voice-box
& stenciled each scream
each prayer
every hymn
in two columns
on my back creating
wordy wings

I am diving down to un-drown you
trying to re-crown you on land again

Listen, I'm telling you
I have cracked it (yoked the sky)
tugged on a leather jacket & John Henry'ed
the seams of it
cut each star in half
& ate the light of it

I glow with it—
gorged vast
Jonah'ed the whale of it
in one gulp became it
   a tall tale
cloudy as mystical seafoam
look at me
look at me
I've grown them
(wings)

⁂ ⁂ ⁂ ⁂

Outro: This poem draws from many folktales, including John Henry (the steel-driving man), Jonah and the whale, and the stories of African Americans growing wings and flying back to Africa. The poem investigates how to get back to Africa, to reverse time, to undo the injustices of slavery. The poem grapples with the impossible task—fixing something that can't be fixed. The only solution—magic. Growing wings.

Track 7: why the mosquito buzzes in your ear

Danez Smith

back when we

all spoke the tongue of the earth

she told a lie   soft as butterfly wings

but lies   stick like old honey

and roll around   picking up anything

on the ground   or right out the low air

and her pretty little lie tricked the iguana
who acted a fool
which scared the snake
who caused a panic
which sent every animal running like wildfire
which shocked the elephants
who shook the earth
which frightened the lions
who freaked gazelles

who rushed the field
which held the trees
and rattled the branches

and down fell the owl child

down the shaking earth

and under a brief sky of hooves

he flew no more

and so the mosquito
whizzes by the ears   of anyone

speaking loud as two suns   or whispering into midnight
trying to hear

if the world has forgotten   the little owl
crushed by her little lie

her wings crying
                                   her bloody apologies

꙳ ꙳ ꙳ ꙳

Outro: It is a truth universally known that seemingly small actions can have profound consequences, and this poem inspects this truth. A tiny lie can cause pain, destruction, violence, and even death. The poem serves as a cautionary tale about the power of our words. This sentiment resonates even more in the Black community, where lies have historically led to tragedy for Black individuals.

Track 8: Grandmother Goddess

L. Renée

A crown of ashen waves gleamed limp from her scalp
as a cascade of silky locs, like the silver tinsel
she hung round the ol' Christmas tree.
Wrinkles on her forehead formed mountains
capped by brown sugar peaks, elevating wisdom
as adventure worth the seek. Glittering gold patches
seemed as sunflower fields along her jade-roped veins
that were speed bumps, kissing scorned boils brewing
on the map of her hands. Brewing, baring the remnants
of a stubborn, rugged, wooden washing board that left
splinters in your pinkie if you caught it against the grain.
Lye soap burning. Igniting layers of skin. Brilliant bursts
blistering as buds of raspberries. No matter to a woman
who logged people's laundry in pounds, not loads. Her eyes,
mahogany windows, gleamed every time she looked
at someone. Her gaze spoke of triumph. A secret held against
all the world that a rock-studded path did not sink her.
She trudged on grandly for all to see she was a Goddess,
undoubtedly. Capturing compassion in her arms, always
  extended,

opened to others as her heart was toward giving—even if
that meant sacrificing necessities she would never acknowledge.
A Goddess, who believed your life is what you make of it.
"And what you make of it is a gift from God," she said once,
winking, wide mouth cracked open, her thirty pearl teeth
   lined up
neatly as if on a necklace string. The missing molars
got in phantom formation the way Black girls becoming
women make something out of nothing. Call it beauty.
Name it special. Say her name: Goddess.
Undoubtedly. And I've got the rivers
of my Grandmother Goddess
flowing through me.

⁂ ⁂ ⁂ ⁂

Outro: In this ode, the speaker clearly sees their grandmother as a
goddess. A woman of immeasurable strength, fortitude, and love. The
poet goes so far as to say, *And I've got the rivers / of my Grandmother
Goddess / flowing through me.* Through imagery that feels almost
dreamlike and metaphors that hint at the infinite nature of stars
and the grandeur of mountains, we see a woman larger than life
and highlight the importance of the matriarch in Black culture.

Track 9: Black Mythology

Jonny Teklit

Under the cover of night, Icarus,
careful not to wake his captors from sleep,
flees from the prison built by his father's
master. He does not look back. He does not
stop. Just as Icarus arrives at the border
of the sky, more North than he's ever thought
possible, Master's son, with blazing rage,
strikes the wings from Icarus' shoulders with a whip,
a tendril of flame hungry for dark meat.

Icarus plummets into the river and drowns.
The river carries him and spits him out
someplace colder, some unfamiliar South,
where he'll tread forever in an ocean
always bloated blue with bodies of kin.

Outro: This sonnet uses the myth of Icarus and infuses it with the Black American experience. In this retelling, Icarus loses his wings because of the whip that is "hungry for dark meat." This Black Icarus is wingless, battered, and roaming because he was stolen from his home.

 **Coda**

We Write

Nikki Giovanni

Writing is a frozen
Thought brought
To paper heated
By passions tempered
By sympathy defined
By facts colored
By desire

Words landing
On pages scramble
To arrange thoughts
Giggle and say exactly
What they want ignoring
Us the writers

Our job is to tame
These words
To train them to perform
Properly and should they
Be unable to actually do
The job at least
Come to work
On time and offer
Proper apologies
When they fall short

We learn to negotiate
The space between
Imagination and possibility
Reality and probability
We mold the world
Into our thoughts
Our thoughts mold
Us into a different
Perspective

We seek and hide
We break and mend
We teach and learn
We write

 BIOGRAPHIES

Producers

Amber McBride is currently an assistant professor at the University of Virginia. She received her MFA in poetry from Emerson College in 2012. Her poetry has appeared in various literary magazines, including *Ploughshares*, *Provincetown Arts*, *Willow Springs*, *The Cincinnati Review*, *The Rumpus*. Her debut YA novel in verse, *Me (Moth)*, was a finalist for the Morris Award and National Book Award for Young People's Literature and won the John Steptoe–Coretta Scott King Award. Her sophomore novel in verse, *We Are All So Good at Smiling*, received five starred reviews. McBride's middle grade novel, *Gone Wolf*, and debut poetry collection, *Thick with Trouble*, are forthcoming.

Taylor Byas (she/her) is a Black Chicago native currently living in Cincinnati, Ohio. She is the first-place winner of the 2020 Poetry Super Highway, the 2020 Frontier Poetry Award for New Poets, and the 2021 Adrienne Rich Award for Poetry. She is the author of the chapbooks *Bloodwarm* and *Shutter* and her debut full-length collection, *I Done Clicked My Heels Three*

Times (2023). She is also a coeditor of the forthcoming *The Southern Poetry Anthology, Volume X: Alabama.*

Erica Martin is a freelance editor and a poet. Her debut poetry collection, *And We Rise*, was released in 2022. It was an ABA Indies Introduce selection, as well as an ABA Indie Next pick. She has been featured by *Oprah Daily* and enjoys making a difference in the world through political activism, reading, and writing. When she's not reading and writing, you can find her editing, baking pies, or watching *The Vampire Diaries* for the millionth time.

Contributing Artists

Kwame Alexander is a poet, educator, producer, and #1 *New York Times* bestselling author of thirty-six books, including *The Door of No Return*; *An American Story*, illustrated by Dare Coulter; *Becoming Muhammad Ali*, coauthored with James Patterson; *Rebound*, which was shortlisted for the prestigious UK Carnegie Medal; the Caldecott Medal– and Newbery Honor–winning picture book, *The Undefeated*, illustrated by Kadir Nelson; and his Newbery Medal–winning middle grade novel, *The Crossover*.

Lauren K. Alleyne hails from the twin island nation of Trinidad and Tobago. Her fiction, poetry, and nonfiction have been widely published in journals and anthologies, including *The Atlantic*, *Ms. Muse*, *Women's Studies Quarterly*, *Interviewing the Caribbean*, and *Crab Orchard Review*, among many others. She is the author of *Difficult Fruit* (2014) and *Honeyfish* (2018).

Jabari Asim is an accomplished poet, playwright, and writer. He has been described as one of the most influential African American literary critics of his generation. Jabari has served as the editor-in-chief of *Crisis* magazine—the NAACP's flagship journal of politics, culture, and ideas. He is the recipient of a Guggenheim Fellowship in Creative Arts and is the author of seven books for adults, including *The N Word* and *We Can't Breathe*. He has also written eleven books for children, including *Fifty Cents and a Dream* and *A Child's Introduction to African American History*. At Emerson College, he is both the graduate program director and director of the MFA program in the Department of Writing, Literature, and Publishing.

Mahogany L. Browne is the executive director of Just Media and the artistic director of Urban Word, and a writer, playwright, organizer, and educator. She was selected as a Kennedy Center Next 50 and a Wesleyan 2022–23 writer in residence and is the first ever poet in residence at Lincoln Center. Browne has received fellowships from Arts for Justice, Serenbe, Cave Canem, Poets House, Mellon Research, and Rauschenberg. She is the author of *Vinyl Moon*, *Chlorine Sky*, *Woke: A Young Poet's Call to Justice*, *Woke Baby*, and *Black Girl Magic*.

DeeSoul Carson (he/they) is a Black queer poet, performer, and educator from San Diego, California. He is a Watering Hole Writing Workshop Fellow, and his work has been featured in Button Poetry, Write About Now Poetry, *The Adroit Journal*, and elsewhere. He graduated with a degree in cultural/social psychology and a minor in creative writing from Stanford University. He is a Writers in the Public Schools Fellow in the NYU MFA program. Find more of his work at deesoulpoetry.com.

Courtne Comrie is always on the search for opportunities to use her voice and writing to encourage others, particularly young people. Her work has been published in PEN America's anthology *Dreaming Out Loud: Voices of Undocumented Students* (2019). Often seeking ways to support and mentor at-risk youth through various programs in her city of residence (Mount Vernon, New York), she is also currently a middle school English teacher at MS 244 in the Bronx, New York. Courtne credits her love of verse being birthed through her own traumas and struggles with mental health. Her debut middle grade novel in verse, *Rain Rising* (2022), and its companion, *Rain Remembers* (2023), received multiple starred reviews.

Ama Asantewa Diaka's poetry has appeared in print (*Ehalakasa Anthology* [2011], *Collected* [2019]) and online in *Litro* magazine, and was long listed for the BN Poetry Award in 2015. Her fiction has appeared in *The Missing Slate*, was shortlisted for the Writivism Prize in 2016, and appeared in *Selves* (an Afro anthology of creative nonfiction) in 2018. Akashic published her chapbook *You Too Will Know Me* in 2019. She just completed an MFA at the Art Institute of Chicago. Her debut poetry collection, *Woman, Eat Me Whole* was published in 2023.

Ryan Douglass is an author, poet, and freelance writer from Atlanta, Georgia. His work on race, literacy, sexuality, and media representation has appeared in the *Huffington Post*, *Atlanta Black*

Star, Everyday Feminism, Nerdy POC, *Age of Awareness, LGBTQ Nation*, and *Medium*, among others. His debut novel, *The Taking of Jake Livingston* (2022), is a YA horror.

Antwan Eady grew up in Garnett, South Carolina, where he spent most of his days riding four-wheelers, fishing, and imagining a world without limitations. Eady is the founder of #BlackCreatorsInKidLit, which aims to bridge the gap between publishing professionals and Black creators (authors and illustrators). When he isn't writing, he's searching for the best Low-Country boil in Savannah, Georgia, where he currently resides.

Kandace Fuller is an up-and-coming writer and an artist. She has always been drawn to the detailed, magical concepts in young adult and middle grade works, which shows in both her writing and illustrations. In her free time, she enjoys reading, traveling, and learning as many languages as she can.

Dr. Joanne V. Gabbin is the director and founder of the Furious Flower Poetry Center, which is the nation's first academic center for Black poetry. Furious Flower was founded in 1994 and has been offering support to Black poets for over twenty years. Dr. Gabbin has devoted her life to uplifting and honoring Black poets. She has edited several anthologies, including *The Furious Flowering of African American Poetry* and *Furious Flower: African American Poetry from the Black Arts Movement to the Present*. Her essays are also widely published. Dr. Gabbin is currently a professor at James Madison University.

Nikki Giovanni is a household name and one of the most well-known poets in America. Her career has been long and bountiful—she is the author of over thirty books, including three *New York Times* bestsellers. She has been nominated for a Grammy and a National Book Award. Nikki Giovanni has won a Langston Hughes Medal and seven NAACP Image Awards. She has written several children's books, including *Spin a Soft Black Song* and *Ego-Tripping and Other Poems for Young People*. Nikki Giovanni was also named one of Oprah Winfrey's twenty-five Living Legends. She is currently a University Distinguished Professor at Virginia Tech.

Faylita Hicks (she/they) is a queer Afro-Latinx activist, writer, and interdisciplinary artist. They are the author of *HoodWitch* (2019), a finalist for the 2020 Lambda Literary Award for Bisexual Poetry; the forthcoming poetry collection *A Map of My Want* (2024); and the debut memoir about their carceral experiences, *A Body of Wild Light* (2025).

Jeanine Jones is a small P.E.A. (poet, author, educator) in a big pot. The Chicago, Illinois, native has made Memphis, Tennessee, her home. Cultural development, the arts, and literacy are important factors in her work. She continuously strives to develop new strategies that are effective for struggling readers. Her absolute affinity for literature, especially poetry, propels her to teach and constantly learn. She attributes her early love of reading and the arts to her parents. They made it possible for her to experience and live life creatively. "Literacy is life—live!" is her motto.

Tony Keith Jr. is an award-winning spoken-word poet, educator, and nerd who writes, reads, and performs about topics dealing with love, liberation, and racial equity in education. He is the recipient of the 2018 DC Commission on the Arts and Humanities Fellowship Award, and his coauthored book *Open Mic Night* received the 2018 Outstanding Book Recognition Award from the American Educational Research Association. Tony is an educational consultant, spoken-word artist, and urban youth development practitioner with over fifteen years of experience leading teams that serve marginalized youth and young adults in schools, colleges, and communities around the world. His debut YA novel in verse, *How the Boogeyman Became a Poet*, is forthcoming.

Simone Liggins earned her MFA in writing at the Jack Kerouac School of Disembodied Poetics of Naropa University. Her work has been featured in *Raven Chronicles*, *Buddy. a lit zine*, *BEATS Periodical*, *Boulder Weekly*, *Outsider Poetry*, and others.

Rodrick Minor is a poet from Mississippi. He is a four-time member of the Baton Rouge National Poetry Slam Team, a member of the Philadelphia National Poetry Slam Team, a Watering Hole Fellow, a Winter Tangerine Workshop alumnus, and a Hurston/Wright Fellow. His writing centers around the study of Afro-gastronomy and how it interacts with identity, religion, mortality, and culture overall.

Jamar J. Perry is the author of the Cameron Battle middle grade fantasy series, published by Bloomsbury. Jamar attended Berea College in Berea, Kentucky, majoring in psychology, English literature, and education. Jamar became a middle school teacher in the Washington, DC, area, hoping to instruct the next generation of scholars, thinkers, and writers. He is currently finishing up his PhD, focusing his research on Black boys, the history of traditional and Black masculinity in America, and racial literacy.

Joy Priest is the author of *HORSEPOWER* (Pitt Poetry Series, 2020), winner of the Donald Hall Prize for Poetry. She is the recipient of the 2020 Stanley Kunitz Memorial Prize, and her poems have appeared in *APR*, *The Atlantic*, and *Poetry Northwest*, among others. Her essays have appeared in *The Bitter Southerner*, *Poets & Writers*, *ESPN*, and *The Undefeated*, and her work has been anthologized in *Breakbeat Poets: New American Poetry in the Age of Hip-Hop*, *The Louisville Anthology*, and *Best New Poets* 2014, 2016, and 2019. Priest has facilitated writing workshops and arbitration programs with adult and juvenile incarcerated women. She is currently a doctoral student in literature and creative writing at the University of Houston.

L. Renée is a poet and nonfiction writer living in Harrisonburg, Virginia, where she works as assistant director of the Furious Flower Poetry Center and is assistant professor of English at James Madison University. She has been nominated for *Best New Poets*, Best of the Net, and a Pushcart Prize, and her work has been published in *Obsidian*, *Tin House Online*, *Poetry Northwest*, and elsewhere. The granddaughter of proud Black Appalachians, she won the international 2022 Rattle Poetry Prize and *Appalachian Review*'s Denny C. Plattner Award, among others. She earned an MFA in creative writing from Indiana University and an MS in journalism from Columbia University.

Sonia Sanchez—poet, activist, scholar—was the Laura Carnell Professor of English and Women's Studies at Temple University. She is the recipient of both the Robert Frost Medal for distinguished lifetime service to American poetry and the Langston Hughes Poetry Award. One of the most important writers of the Black arts movement, Sanchez is the author of sixteen books.

Danez Smith is the author of three collections, including *Homie* and *Don't Call Us Dead*. They have won the Forward Prize for Best Collection, the Minnesota Book Award in Poetry, the Lambda

Literary Award for Gay Poetry, The Kate Tufts Discovery Award, and have been a finalist for the NAACP Image Award in Poetry and the National Book Award.

Originally from Chicagoland, **Fatima Stephens** has written fiction all her life. Her fascination with horror and all things supernatural has greatly influenced her work.

Jonny Teklit is a winner of the 2019 Academy of American Poets College Poetry Prize, as well as the recipient of the 2019 Aliki Perroti and Seth Frank Most Promising Young Poet Award. His work has appeared in *The New Yorker*, *The Adroit Journal*, *Catapult*, *Alien Magazine*, *Glass Poetry Press*, *Mixed Mag*, *Dishsoap Quarterly*, *The Susquehanna Review*, and elsewhere.

Tariq Thompson's poetry has appeared in the *American Poetry Review*, *The Adroit Journal*, *Sixth Finch*, *wildness*, and *Poemhood: Our Black Revival*. Thompson won the Adroit Prize for poetry in 2020 and is a finalist for a 2023 Ruth Lilly and Dorothy Sargent Rosenberg Poetry Fellowship. Thompson received his BA in English from Kenyon College and is completing his MFA at New York University.

Donald Vincent (aka Mr. Hip) is a poet, educator, and musician. He can now be found teaching English composition for UCLA's writing programs and literature at Emerson College, Los Angeles. Donald enjoys using storytelling as an instrument for change and advancing an understanding of justice and compassion. His debut poetry collection, *Convenient Amnesia*, was published in 2020.

Ashley Woodfolk has loved reading and writing for as long as she can remember. She graduated from Rutgers University and worked in children's book publishing for over a decade. Now a full-time mom and writer, Ashley lives in a sunny Brooklyn apartment with her cute husband, her cuter dog, and the cutest baby in the world. Her books include *The Beauty That Remains*, *When You Were Everything*, *Blackout*, and the Flyy Girls series.

Ibi Zoboi is the *New York Times* bestselling author of *American Street*, a National Book Award finalist; *Pride*, a contemporary remix of Jane Austen's *Pride and Prejudice*; and her middle grade debut, *My Life as an Ice Cream Sandwich*. Zoboi is also the author of *Nigeria Jones* and *Star Child: A Biographical Constellation of Octavia Estelle Butler*. She coauthored the Walter Award and L.A. Times Book Prize–winning novel in verse, *Punching the Air*, with Yusef Salaam. Her debut picture book, *The People Remember*, received a Coretta Scott King Honor Award.

The OGs (Ancestors)

James Baldwin (1924–1987) was born in Harlem and would go on to become a prominent essayist, poet, novelist, and a leading voice in the civil rights movement. In his novels he highlighted the difficulty of being Black in the United States. *The Fire Next Time* and *Go Tell It on the Mountain* are two of his well-known novels.

Gwendolyn Brooks (1917–2000) was born in Topeka, Kansas, on June 7, to David Anderson Brooks, the son of a runaway slave, and Keziah Corinne (née Wims), and raised in Chicago. Brooks began writing poetry in her teenage years and published her first poem in *American Childhood* magazine. Brooks also became a regular contributor to the *Chicago Defender*'s "Lights and Shadows" poetry column when she was sixteen. Brooks was the author of more than twenty books of poetry.

Lucille Clifton's (1936–2010) many children's books, written expressly for an African American audience, include *All Us Come Cross the Water* (1973), *Three Wishes* (1976), and *My Friend Jacob* (1980). She also wrote an award-winning series of books featuring events in the life of Everett Anderson, a young Black boy. Clifton served as poet laureate of Maryland from 1979–85.

Langston Hughes (1901–1967) was a leader of the Harlem Renaissance. His first collection of poetry, *Weary Blues*, was published in 1926 and his first novel, *Not Without Laughter*, was published in 1930 shortly after he graduated from college. Hughes would go on to write brilliant works, including eleven plays, that artfully captured being Black in America during the 1920s to 1960s.

Etheridge Knight (1931–1991) was born in Corinth, Mississippi. He dropped out of school as soon as he could join the army and served for four years in Korea before returning home. Knight did not start writing poetry until 1965, when he was serving an eight-year sentence at the Indiana State Prison. His poetry investigated addiction, generational trauma, the experience of being a Black man in a racist society, and the importance of community. While he was incarcerated, poets like Gwendolyn Brooks and Dudley Randall would visit him. Knight became a leading voice of the Black arts movement.

Audre Lorde (1934–1992), who wrote in both prose and verse, addressed racism, homophobia, identity, and classism in her work. Some of her most well-known collections include *Cables to Rage* (1970), *The Black Unicorn*, and *From a Land Where Other People Live*. Lorde was also a leading voice in the civil rights and LGBTQ rights movements and wrote prolifically on these topics for her entire life. Lorde identified as a Black lesbian and often introduced herself as a *Black, feminist, lesbian, poet, mother, and activist.*

Claude McKay (1889-1948) was born in Jamaica and always fostered a love for poetry. In 1912, after the publication of his first book, *Song of Jamaica*, he traveled to South Carolina, and then Alabama to attend the Tuskegee Institute. He continued to write poetry, *Harlem Shadows* (1922), and fiction but much of his work was actually published after his death. McKay wrote honestly about the Black experience in the United States and abroad, often speaking on racism and economic inequality. His work made him a leading voice of the Harlem Renaissance.

Originally from West Africa, **Phillis Wheatley** (1753–1784) was stolen from her home around the age of seven and brought to Boston where she was enslaved by an affluent family. She was a curious child and was taught how to read and write. She became a well-known poet, with her work first being published in London. She was eventually emancipated and continues to be known as the first Black published poet. She enjoyed writing in form and often wrote about religion and spirituality.

Permissions

"Go Gator and Muddy the Water" by Zora Neale Hurston, part of "Works-in-Progress for the Florida Negro," in *Zora Neale Hurston: Folklore, Memoirs, and Other Writings*, ed. Cheryl Wall (New York: Library of America, 1995), p. 875. Used with approval of the Zora Neale Hurston Trust.

"Young Afrikans" copyright © 1987 by Gwendolyn Brooks, from *Blacks* (Chicago: Third World Press, 1987). Reprinted by consent of Brooks Permissions.

"Power" from *The Collected Poems of Audre Lorde*. Copyright © 1978 by Audre Lorde. Used by permission of W. W. Norton & Company, Inc.

"The South" copyright © 2024 by Halcyenda Erica Martin

"Colors" copyright © 2024 by Fatima Stephens

"Textured" copyright © 2024 by Kandace Fuller

"10:32pm" copyright © 2024 by Courtne Comrie

"Views for Damani" copyright © 2024 by Anthony R. Keith, Jr.

"Greasy Butt Kids" copyright © 2024 by Dr. Joanne V. Gabbin

"Like a Wildfire" copyright © 2024 by Ashley Woodfolk

"won't you celebrate with me" copyright © 1993 by Lucille Clifton, from *The Book of Light*. Reprinted with the permission of The Permissions Company, LLC on behalf of Copper Canyon Press, coppercanyonpress.org.

"Douen" copyright © 2024 by Lauren K. Alleyne

"Genesis" by Etheridge Knight, from *The Essential Etheridge Knight*. Copyright © 1986. Used by permission of the University of Pittsburgh Press.

"Exodus" copyright © 2024 by Jamar J. Perry